Advent Storybook

By *Antonie Schneider*

Illustrated by
Maja Dusíková

Translated by Marisa Miller

North South

Copyright © 2004 by NordSüd Verlag AG, CH-8050 Zürich, Switzerland.
First published in Switzerland under the title *Wann ist endlich Weihnachten?*
English translation copyright © 2005 by NorthSouth Books Inc., New York 10016.

First published in the United States, Great Britain, Canada, Australia, and New Zealand in 2005
by NorthSouth Books Inc., an imprint of NordSüd Verlag AG, CH-8050 Zürich, Switzerland.
Distributed in the United States by NorthSouth Books Inc., New York 10016.

Library of Congress Cataloging-in-Publication Data is available.
A CIP catalogue record for this book is available from The British Library.
ISBN: 978-0-7358-1963-4 (trade edition)
15 17 19 • 20 18 16 14

Printed in Latvia by Livonia Print, Riga, 2018.

www.northsouth.com

For our children, and for all who are
on their way to Bethlehem —A. S.

Benjamin Bear was tucked in his warm bed, but he couldn't fall asleep.

"When will Christmas finally be here?" he asked Mother Bear.

"You have to be patient, Benjamin," said Mother. "But tomorrow you can open the first door on your Advent calendar, and we will begin our journey to Bethlehem."

"How far is it to Bethlehem?" asked Benjamin.

Mother Bear smiled. "24 stories away!"

"And then it's really Christmas?"

Mother Bear nodded and gave Benjamin a big kiss on the nose. "Good night, now, little one."

The Star with a Tail

On December 1st, *just before bed, Benjamin Bear opened the first door on the Advent calendar. "Oh, look—a star with a tail!" he cried.*

Once upon a time there was a little bear just like you. He discovered a star one night shining in the sky above his cave. He had never seen such a bright star before. It was a very special star indeed because the little bear, full of curiosity, felt compelled to follow it.

He ran over hills and mountains, swam across a wide river, and climbed the steepest rocks. But the little bear finally got so tired that he had to stop and rest. He lay down and fell fast asleep. When he awoke, he sprang up in a panic. "My star! Where is my star? I lost my star!" he cried.

How surprised he was to see the tail of the star shining brighter than the sun. The little bear set out again, relieved and even more determined to follow the wondrous star.

When Mother Bear finished the story, Benjamin pointed to the star. "Look at it shine!" he said happily.

"Yes," said Mother. "Remember that God is with you night and day to show you the way."

The Eagle

On December 2nd, *Benjamin opened the next door and uncovered an eagle.*

After the little bear had walked for many hours, he saw a very young eagle sitting in his nest on top of the highest cliff.

"What are you looking at?" the little bear asked the young eagle.

"I keep watching that star. It seems to be calling to me. I wish I could follow it."

"When you learn how to fly, you can follow it," said the mother eagle.

The young eagle thought for a while. "Then I must learn to fly right away!" he said.

"I will show you," said his mother. "You're big enough." Then she threw the young eagle out of the nest.

The little bear screamed in horror. But before the young eagle struck the ground, the mother eagle swooped down and caught him, then carried him back up to the nest. Over and over again, the mother eagle dropped him from the nest, then caught him in her wings.

The little bear watched eagerly as the little eagle suddenly spread his wings wide and flew higher and higher until he disappeared in the direction of the star.

"Wait!" cried the little bear. "I'm following the star, too." And he hurried on his way.

"Does the mother eagle always catch her young when they fall?" asked Benjamin when his mother finished the story.

"If we trust in God, he will always catch us before we fall," Mother Bear replied and gave Benjamin a big hug.

The Blind Man

On December 3rd *Benjamin opened the next door and saw a blind man.*

As the little bear wandered over the countryside one night, he saw a flame in the distance. As he stepped closer, he could make out a man with a burning torch in his hand.

"Who are you?" the little bear asked the stranger.

"I am a blind man," said the man, "and am following the glorious star."

"But how can you find the way?" asked the little bear, amazed.

The blind man smiled and said, "Do you see my torch?"

"Yes," replied the little bear.

"Everyone who sees my torch accompanies me for a bit," said the blind man.

The little bear timidly grasped the man's large hand and led him along the path. Above them, the star seemed to shine even brighter, making the journey easier.

When Mother Bear finished the story, she lit a lantern and placed it in the window. "If you are ever lost in the dark, Benjamin," she said, "remember that this light will be shining to help you find your way home."

The Giant

On December 4th, *Benjamin opened the next door and saw a giant.*

For three days and three nights the little bear followed the star. It was a long way to Bethlehem. His path led him through a deep forest. Suddenly, the little bear heard music. He sat down to rest, leaning back against the trunk of a tree, listening to the music. He thought longingly of his soft, warm bed at home. The music faded and the tree trunk moved.

"Hey, you." The rumble came from behind him. "You're sitting on my leg!"

Startled, the little bear jumped up. "A giant," he stammered. "W-w-what are you doing here?"

"I'm practicing!" said the giant. "Don't disturb me!" He picked up his harmonica and continued playing.

"What are you practicing for?" asked the little bear.

"I have heard that a Child will be born in Bethlehem. People call him the King of Kings. I must find a special star to guide me so I can go to the Child and play my most beautiful song for him."

"I've seen that star," said the little bear.

"The star with the tail? Then show it to me!" The giant lifted the little bear onto his back and walked through the dark forest.

The little bear pointed proudly to the sky. "See how my star shines!"

The giant jerked to a halt. "That's the one!" he cried loudly. Then he lifted the startled little bear down from his shoulders and ran off.

"The little bear helped the big giant, didn't he, Mother?" said Benjamin.

"Yes," Mother Bear replied. "Even the small and weak can help those bigger and stronger to find their way."

The Ant

On December 5th, *Benjamin opened the next door and found a little ant.*

The little bear continued his long, long journey. Sometimes when he felt tired or discouraged he would look up and see a little black dot in the sky. It was the eagle following the star, and it cheered the little bear and gave him energy to continue.

In the middle of a field the little bear discovered a large anthill. The ants all stopped work to greet him—all except for one ant who was busy leveling a large pile of sand one grain at a time. The little bear watched her in amazement. "Why are you doing that?" he asked.

"My friend is at the bottom of this pile!"

"I would be glad to help you," said the little bear.

"No, no! Your paws are much too big," said the ant. "You could hurt my friend."

"Ant," said the little bear, "you will never remove the sand pile by yourself, even if you live to be 100 years old."

The ant paused for a moment, then said, "I am going to try to save my friend anyway." And she continued to work.

Suddenly there was movement among the other ants. They had been listening. The little bear watched as the ants began to help, each carrying off one grain of sand at a time. Before long, the entire pile was gone and a little ant crawled out safe and sound!

"That was amazing!" said Benjamin.

"You see, Benjamin," said Mother Bear, "faith can move mountains."

The Man in Red

On December 6th, *Benjamin opened the next door and saw a man in red.*

It grew darker and darker. The path to Bethlehem seemed immeasurably long to the little bear. Snowflakes blew in his face. He closed his eyes for a moment. He was so sleepy. . . .

The little bear yawned. Before him stood a man dressed in red, with a large sack slung over his back, leading a donkey.

"Hello there, little bear. My name is Nicholas. What are you doing out on such a cold night?"

"I am following the star to Bethlehem to see the Child that will be born," muttered the bear.

Nicholas smiled. "Then we are going the same way!" he said. Without waiting for a reply, he lifted the little bear onto his donkey. When they reached a village, the little bear saw children peering out of brightly lit windows. What are they waiting for, he wondered. Then he saw empty plates and boots in front of the doors.

Nicholas opened his large sack. It was filled with apples, nuts, and gingerbread. "Will you help me, little bear?"

The little bear nodded and cheerfully passed out all the goodies. "Now the sack is empty!" said the bear, disappointed. "We've given away everything."

"And because we did, we are nearer to Bethlehem," replied Nicholas. . . .

The little bear rubbed his eyes. It was morning. The sun was shining. Next to him lay a small sack with a card that read, for the little bear.

"I'm glad the little bear got some goodies, too," said Benjamin.

"Yes," agreed Mother Bear. "But remember that sharing with others brings us closer to God."

The Rosebush

On December 7th, Benjamin opened the next door and found a rosebush.

That night the snowflakes fell like gigantic stars. With tremendous effort, the little bear fought his way through the deep snow. His fur was wet, and he shivered. The little bear sank deeper and deeper into the snow. In front of him lay a little clearing. He squinted and saw something sparkling just ahead. The little bear bent down. He could hardly believe his eyes. In the middle of winter a rose was blooming! The ice crystals sparkled and glistened on its leaves.

It is so beautiful, thought the little bear. I will dig it out and bring it to the Child! His little paws scraped away the snow. He dug his claws into the frost-hardened earth until they were dull. Finally he was able to pull out the rosebush by its roots. He pressed the rosebush, stiff with frost, against his chest and warmed it.

Just then, a flock of birds flew by and began to sing. And, as if it were already spring, the rose released its sweet scent into the woods.

"A rose blooming in winter! That must have been wonderful to see," said Benjamin.

Mother Bear nodded. "Always remember," she said, "God's love can warm and brighten the coldest, darkest night."

The Beggar

On December 8th, *Benjamin opened the next door and saw a beggar.*

The snowflakes fell even more heavily. It was harder and harder for the little bear to find his way. As he stumbled through the drifts, he came across a man dressed in rags.

What a poor man, thought the little bear. He looks so hungry! He held out his sack filled with goodies and offered it to the man. "I was going to give this to the Child who will be born in Bethlehem," the little bear explained, "but I think you need it more."

A smile flickered across the man's face. "He will have some, too!" he said and vanished.

How light the little bear's heart suddenly felt! The road to Bethlehem seemed shorter to him, but he didn't know why.

"Why did the road seem shorter, Mother?" asked Benjamin.

"Helping the needy can lighten our spirits and fill us with energy," *Mother Bear replied.*

The Well

On December 9th, Benjamin opened the next door and saw a well.

The little bear trekked across a desert. The sand burned his feet and he was desperately thirsty. With his last ounce of strength he dragged himself to a well, but it was empty. Only mud and dirt lay at the bottom.

"I'll die of thirst," groaned the little bear. And he felt very alone. Then, in the distance, he heard a loud jumble of voices. He could see a magnificently decorated caravan moving across the dunes.

"Have pity! Take me with you!" the little bear called out and sank back down, exhausted.

But no one heard him.

While the little bear slept in the hot sand, three men dressed like kings came and filled the well to the brim with water. Then they got back on their camels and moved on.

A small mouse had seen everything. She tugged the little bear's ear. "Wake up! There is water in the well again!"

It took all the little bear's strength to drag himself to the well. He drank and drank until he was no longer thirsty.

Meanwhile, a fox and a snake had come over, curious to see what had happened. "A miracle took place in the desert!" they whispered in astonishment. "Look! Flowers are blooming all around the well!"

And the little bear, filled with renewed strength, continued on his way.

"I'm so glad the little bear didn't die of thirst," said Benjamin.

"So am I," said Mother Bear. "You see, Benjamin, God always hears our calls for help."

The Pear Tree

On December 10th, *Benjamin opened the next door and saw a pear tree.*

The little bear saw a pear tree at the edge of the path. I'd like to rest in its shade for a bit, he thought, and leaned against its gnarled trunk.

When the little bear woke from a light slumber, he looked up and saw that the old tree was full of ripe fruit.

"I am so hungry!" the little bear said with a sigh. "If only I could eat some of your fruit!"

As if the old pear tree had understood his words, it tilted its crown right down to the ground. The little bear picked many luscious pears, which tasted like the sweetest honey. When he was full, the pear tree raised its crown with a rustle.

"Thank you!" cried the little bear and, refreshed, continued on his way.

"I wish I had a pear to eat right now," said Benjamin, licking his lips.

Mother Bear laughed. "We must always be grateful for God's bounty," she said.

The Angel

On December 11th, *Benjamin opened the next door and uncovered an angel.*

The little bear awoke the next night from a strange dream. He saw an angel walking on the path ahead of him.

"Where are you going?" asked the little bear.

"To Bethlehem!" answered the angel.

It was then that the little bear noticed the angel had only one wing. How hard it must be for the angel, thought the little bear. With one wing she certainly cannot fly!

Suddenly he heard a soft voice behind him. "I, too, have only one wing and want to go to Bethlehem to see the Child that will be born. I have heard that this Child will heal all."

Astounded, the little bear turned toward the voice. "You too?" he cried in surprise.

At that very moment, the two angels linked arms and cried happily, "How wonderful to have found one another—now we can fly to Bethlehem together!"

"I wonder how those angels lost their wings," said Benjamin.

"I don't know," said Mother Bear. "But it's nice to know that God gives us friends and loved ones to help us on our journey."

The Lamb

On December 12th, *Benjamin opened the next door and found a lamb.*

As the little bear set out again early in the morning, he sighed, "Bethlehem is so far!" he said. Just then he saw a little lamb.

"What are you doing here all alone?" asked the little bear.

"Oh," replied the little lamb, "I am hiding. I'm so afraid of the cow with her sharp horns, the eagle with his powerful talons, even your sharp claws, little bear. I have no horns or talons or claws—no strengths to defend myself with."

The little bear looked up at his star. "You are gentle and kind and patient, little lamb. Those are your great strengths."

The little bear stroked the little lamb lovingly on the head. "Come along with me, won't you?" he asked, and together they continued on.

"Do you think the little lamb was really strong enough to defend herself?" asked Benjamin.

"I think so," said Mother Bear. "Gentleness, kindness, and patience are strong weapons indeed."

The Dog

On December 13th, Benjamin opened the next door and uncovered a dog.

Snow covered the valley once more. The lamb and the little bear searched in vain for shelter. Then they discovered red footprints in the snow.

"I hope there are no wolves nearby!" whispered the little lamb, frightened.

They followed the tracks. In a small hut lay a sheepdog, whining softly. When he saw the two, he struggled to stand up.

"What's wrong?" asked the little bear.

The dog howled and licked his left paw.

The little bear examined it carefully. "A thorn!" he declared. "Hold still so I can pull it out."

The dog clenched his teeth and whimpered.

"I got the thorn!" cried the little bear. "Now you can walk again!"

"However can I thank you?" asked the dog.

"By guiding us through the forest and protecting us!" said the little bear.

"Gladly," said the dog and led them safely to the edge of the forest. They thanked him and waved good-bye as the dog trotted back to his little hut.

Mother Bear tickled Benjamin's ear. "You see, Benjamin, a good deed can bring unexpected rewards," she said.

The Robber

On December 14th, *Benjamin opened the next door and found a robber.*

The little bear and the lamb stood at the edge of the forest. They did not see the dangerous robber hiding behind a tree, waiting to kill and rob anyone who passed by. But the robber saw them. They look just right, thought the robber. They'll make me a nice lamb roast and a warm bearskin coat. Just as he was about to pounce on the little bear, the star flashed brightly, blinding the robber who staggered about, screaming, "My eyes! Help! I'm blind!" He fell to the ground.

The little bear knelt and placed his handkerchief over the robber's eyes. "There, there," he said soothingly. "I wish I could stay and help you more, but I must follow the star to Bethlehem to see the Child who will be born. You should come with us, for perhaps the Child can heal you."

Ashamed, the robber grasped the little bear's tiny paw. "Thank you," he said. "I am so sorry. I promise I will never rob or kill again." He walked along beside the bear and the lamb and with every step toward Bethlehem, the darkness receded.

After they had walked together for quite a while, the little bear said, "Your legs are much faster. Go ahead of us—the star will guide you to Bethlehem."

"That was scary!" said Benjamin. "I'm glad the robber didn't get his lamb roast or bearskin coat!"

"Yes," agreed Mother Bear. "And it's nice to know that if we are truly sorry, God always forgives us."

The Cane

On December 15th, Benjamin opened the next door and found a cane.

Sleepily and silently, the lamb and the little bear trudged on, with only the hoot of an owl to break the silence. It grew colder. The howling of the wolves made them walk faster. The little bear was so discouraged. Why had he ever set out on this long journey, he wondered. Maybe he should quit and go home. Suddenly a light pierced the fog. They walked toward it and stopped in front of a small hut. Smoke billowed from the chimney. The little bear knocked timidly on the door.

"Who is there?" asked a woman.

"A lamb and a little bear on the way to Bethlehem!"

The woman opened the door and pointed to a table, laden with food. "I've been expecting you. Come in!"

Astonished, the little bear and lamb sat down at the table and ate until they were full. They lay down by the fireplace and fell fast asleep.

The next morning, they could not find the woman to thank her. And as they stepped out the door and looked back, the house disappeared. All that remained was a cane. The little bear gladly picked it up and continued on his journey.

"It's good the little bear didn't give up and go home," said Benjamin.

"Yes," agreed Mother Bear. "Faith and courage can banish despair."

The Crown

On December 16th, *Benjamin opened the next door and found a crown.*

As the little bear and the lamb wandered through the night, they met a king. He wore a magnificent golden crown, but his robe was torn and his feet were bare.

"Where are you going?" asked the bear.

The king replied, "I want to see the King who will be born to save us all, but I don't know where to find him. I have been wandering for a long time. I want to bring him my crown!"

The little bear stared in amazement. He pointed to his star. "Just follow that star. It will show you the way!"

Then the king with the gold crown hurried off, following the star to Bethlehem.

"How funny," said Benjamin. "The king was lost, wasn't he?"

"Yes," said Mother Bear. "But he found the way. And God welcomes every-one—rich and poor, kings and little lambs alike."

The Precious Stone

On December 17th, *Benjamin opened the next door and uncovered a precious stone.*

Early in the morning the little lamb and the little bear met a man who sat staring at a bright red stone.

"What are you doing?" asked the little bear.

"I'm thinking," said the man. "For many years I've been thinking."

"What about?" asked the little bear.

"I would like to ask you a question, little bear," said the man. "I will give you this precious stone if you can tell me where God lives."

The little bear said nothing for a while. Then he said quietly, "I will give you this precious rosebush if you can tell me where God does not live."

The man looked at the little bear for a long time. "Little bear," he finally said, "you are very wise. Where are you headed?"

"To Bethlehem, where a new King is to be born," answered the bear.

"I wish I could go, too," said the man," but one of my legs is far too weak." With effort he stood up and limped a few steps.

"Here!" said the little bear. "This cane is for you! Just follow the star. You'll make it, I'm sure."

Benjamin sighed happily.

Mother Bear patted him gently. "The little bear was very wise," she said. "God does live everywhere."

The Bird, the Hare, and the Squirrel

On December 18th, *Benjamin opened the next door and found a bird, a hare, and a squirrel.*

Thick fog covered the countryside. Suddenly there appeared before the lamb and the little bear three animals: a bird, a hare, and a squirrel. The bird could not sing, the hare could not hear despite his large ears, and the squirrel could not jump, for his tail was lame.

"Where are you going?" asked the little bear.

"To someone who can help us!" replied the squirrel. Then the three animals disappeared into the fog.

"I wonder what they mean?" said the bear. But he was very sleepy, so he lay his head on the lamb's back and fell asleep thinking about it.

Then he had a dream.

Above a very poor stable shone the star. Its light slipped through the opening onto the Child lying in a manger. How astonished the bear was to suddenly see the squirrel leaping joyfully around the laughing Child. The bird sang, and the hare kept time with his ears.

The little bear woke from his dream. "Little lamb," he said, "I saw the squirrel, the bird, and the hare in a dream! And they were healthy!"

Rested, they cheerfully went on their way.

"I hope the little bear's dream came true," said Benjamin.

Mother Bear nodded. "His dream was a kind of prayer, and the prayers that please God the most are the ones we pray for others."

The Wolves

On December 19th, *Benjamin Bear opened the next door and uncovered wolves.*

It was nighttime and very quiet. The little bear and the lamb saw a campfire in the distance. As they approached, they saw shepherds sitting around the fire, warming themselves. In the distance they heard the howling of wolves. The shepherds shivered with fear.

"What are you doing here on such a cold night?" asked one of the shepherds.

"We are following the star," replied the little bear.

"What for?" asked the shepherd with a laugh. But then the shepherds suddenly saw their sheep stand up and stare at the heavens. A great light spread across the sky.

"There's the star!" whispered the little bear.

As if led by an invisible shepherd, the sheep set out on the path. The wolves moved with them and did not harm them and, filled with wonder, the lamb, the little bear, and the shepherds hurried behind them all.

"How amazing!" said Benjamin. "The wolves didn't harm them!"

"Yes," said Mother Bear. "God's love can turn enemies into friends."

The Donkey

On December 20th, *Benjamin opened the next door and uncovered a donkey.*

The next morning the little lamb and the little bear walked alone again. Suddenly a donkey rushed up to them. He let out a mournful cry.

"What's the matter?" asked the little bear.

"I lost my song!" moaned the donkey.

"Since when do donkeys sing?" the little bear asked, baffled.

"Since the beginning of the world," replied the donkey sadly and looked at the sky. "What a strange star that is shining in the middle of the day."

"It's the star of Bethlehem. It will find your song for you!" the little bear told the unhappy donkey.

"Do you really think so?" asked the donkey.

The little bear nodded.

The closer they got to the town of Bethlehem, the louder the donkey cried. "Hee-haw, hee-haw, hee-haw!" But to the little bear's ears it sounded like heavenly music.

Benjamin yawned sleepily.

Mother Bear tucked the covers around him tightly. "Good night, Benjamin," she said. "Remember that our faith is music to God's ears."

The Animal Train

On December 21st, Benjamin opened the next door and found a long train of animals.

The next day the little bear and the little lamb came upon a long line of animals. "Watch out," a turtle cried suddenly, annoyed. "I'm in a hurry!"

The little bear had tripped over him in all the excitement. "I'm sorry," he said. "Where are you all hurrying to?"

"To the comfort-giver!" answered the fox. Behind the fox a lion appeared. The little bear trembled with fear.

"Where are you going?" he asked.

"To the protector of the weak!" he answered. On the lion's head sat a pigeon.

The little bear stared in amazement, "Is that what you call the Child who will be born in Bethlehem?" he asked.

The animals nodded.

"Then we have the same destination!" cried the little bear, and he and the lamb joined the long train of animals headed for Bethlehem.

"What is the Child's name, Mother?" asked Benjamin.

Mother Bear smiled. "Oh he has many names. But no matter what we call him what is most important is to worship him."

The Apple Tree

On December 22nd, *Benjamin opened the next door and found an apple tree.*

The little bear and the lamb followed the star into the town of Bethlehem. In a narrow street they noticed a man with a donkey. On the donkey sat a woman. The man stopped at the inn and knocked on the door. "We are seeking shelter," he said.

"I'm sorry, but every last room is full," said the innkeeper. "All I can offer is the stable, just outside of town."

Gratefully, the man and woman set out for the stable.

The little bear's heart thumped loudly in his chest. The woman looked so tired. It made the little bear feel sad. Then, as the couple passed by a winter-bare apple tree, the tree burst into blossom, right before his eyes! The little bear was cheered by the sight. Everything will be all right, he told himself, and followed the couple to the stable.

When Mother Bear finished the story, Benjamin smiled. "The flowering apple tree was a hopeful sign, wasn't it?" he asked.

"Yes, indeed," replied his mother. "Miracles can happen any time."

The Ox

On December 23rd, *Benjamin opened the next door and found an ox.*

The streets of Bethlehem were bustling with activity. The little bear and the lamb were awed by all the people. Suddenly an ox entered the village square. He was large and strong. He wore his horns proudly like a crown. He walked by himself. No one led him. The children ran from him, frightened.

The ox stopped in the middle of the square, bent his knees, and knelt. For a moment the bustle stopped, and everyone knelt with him, filled with wonder.

The lamb and little bear knelt too. Above them the star shone brighter than ever. "I believe we are very close to the Child now," said the little bear.

The ox rose.

"Wait!" cried the little bear.

Then the ox took the little bear and the little lamb on his back. "We must hurry," he said. "The Child will be born very soon and I want to be there to warm him with my breath."

"Does that mean we're almost there now?" asked Benjamin, excitedly.

"Yes indeed!" said Mother Bear. "Do you see how God inspires wonder in us all?"

The Manger

On December 24th, *Benjamin opened the last door and saw a manger.*

As the little bear and the lamb approached the warm stable, they saw the Child lying in a manger. The Child opened his arms to the little bear, laughing.

And the little bear's heart was filled with joy.

Everyone who the little bear had met along the way gathered before the manger: the animals, the beggar, the robber, the old man, the blind man, the king.

And above them all shone the star.

Benjamin sighed happily. "It's finally here, Mother!" he said. "It's finally Christmas!"

Mother Bear kissed Benjamin on the cheek and said . . .

"Merry Christmas!"

About the Author

Antonie Schneider was born in Mindelheim, in southern Germany, where she still lives. A former elementary school teacher, she has written numerous other books for NorthSouth, including *The Dearest Little Mouse in the World, The Birthday Bear, Luke the Lionhearted, Come Back, Pigeon!*, and *Good-Bye, Vivi!*

About the Illustrator

Maja Dusíková was born in Piestany, Czechoslovakia, and now lives in Florence, Italy. She has illustrated many books for both children and adults, including *Mona the Monster Girl; Rapunzel; What Lies on the Other Side?; Good-Bye, Vivi!; The Gift from Saint Nicholas;* and *Silent Night, Holy Night*, all published by NorthSouth.